READ with me!

Kate and
the crocodile

by WILLIAM MURRAY
stories by JILL CORBY
illustrated by STUART TROTTER

Ladybird Books

Tom is at home.
He is in bed.

Sam has a ball.

No, Sam, no.
You can't jump on the bed.

Tom has the ball now.

You can't have it, he says.

Come here, Kate and Tom,
says Mother.

Kate is not here, says Tom.
Kate is in bed.

Tom, tell Kate to come here,
Mother says.

Tell Kate to come here, now.

Come on, Kate and Tom,
says Mother.

Kate, this is for you, she says.
And Tom, this is yours.

Sam, come on and have
yours now, she says.
Come now, Sam.

Here is your hat, Tom,
says Mother.
And here is your hat, Kate.

Kate and Tom,
put your hats on now.

You must put this on
now, Kate.
And Tom, here is yours.

I must have this toy,
says Kate.

We must go to school now,
says Mother.

Here is your lunch box, Kate.
And Tom, here is your lunch box,
she says.

Come on, Kate, we must
go to school now, says Tom.

Kate tells Tom to look.
Look at that, she says.

Come with me, says Mother.
We must go to school.
Come with me now, she says.

Here is the school.
In we go, they say.

Put your hat here,
Tom says to Kate.
And you must put
your lunch box on here.

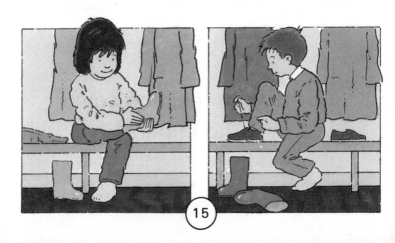

The teacher comes up to
Tom and Kate.

Come with me, she says.
We must go in here.

Tom likes to read.
He looks at the boats.

I like to read, he tells Kate.
He tells the teacher
he likes to read.

Kate, says the teacher,
this is Suki.
Come with me, says Suki.

Come and play with me.
Kate likes to play with Suki.

Can you see this fish, Kate?
Suki says.
See that in the water.
It is like yours.

Look at this toy,
says the teacher.

It's for you to play with, Suki.
Now you can go and play.

They play with the toys.
I can put it in the water,
says Suki.

See that go in the water.
It can go round and round.

Come in now, please,
says the teacher.
Suki and Kate, please come
with your toys.

They all go into school.

Here you are, Kate and Suki.
You can have this.

Can you read it, Suki?
Yes, Suki says, I can read that.

Read that book to Kate,
please, says the teacher.
Yes, read it to me, please, Suki,
says Kate.

Suki reads the book to Kate.
The book says that
we must do it like this.

Can you see? says Suki.
We must put it here.

Here is your lunch box, Kate.
Come with me
to have your lunch.

We go up here.
We all go up here for lunch.

Stay with me, Kate, Suki says.
We stay here to have lunch.

We are all here now.

Do this with the sand,
says Suki.
You can do this with the sand.

There is some water over there,
Kate says.

The toys can stay in
the water and go round and
round, she says.

Now they can go up
over the sand.

Now we can do this, Suki says.
Please come and do this
with me, Kate.

This can go round here,
and that can go over there.

I can just put some sand on
here, and you can put that sand
over there, Kate says.

I can put that up for you now,
says the teacher.
Now we can see all of it.

It can stay up there
for all of you to see.

I can put Tom's rabbits
over here, she says.

We can see all of the rabbits
up there.

We can hop like rabbits,
round and round.

We can hop up here and
we can hop over there.

Rabbits hop like this and
they can hop like that.

I can hop,
just like you.

The teacher says, Just look
at this, just look at
all this sand.

Please put
all of the sand
in there.

The sand must go in
there now.
Wait there, Kate,
and Suki can do it.
She can put it all in there.

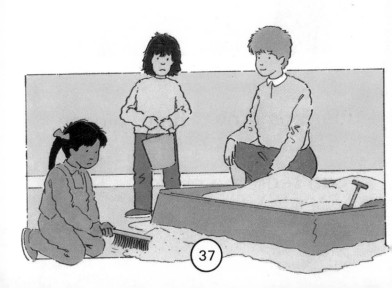

Come here all of you, please,
says the teacher.
I want to read this book to you.

Just come over here, please.
Just stay here with me and
I can read the book.

There are rabbits in this book.
And look at this...

You can all go home now,
says the teacher.
I have your lunch box,
Tom tells Kate.

And your hat is over there.
Wait for me, Kate.
Please wait for me, says Tom.

Look, there is Sam.
Now we can all go home.

Number of words used.............................34

All Key Words are carried forward into the following book, Book 6 *The dream*.

Look at the pictures and read the words.
Which word is missing?

They play with the toys
in the ....

water   fish   sand

Suki reads the
.... to Kate.

boats   book

rabbit

Notes for using this book

The words, pictures and planning of this book are designed to:

* help the child to learn to read
* help you to make learning an exciting and enjoyable experience for her *
* encourage lots of conversation
* help her to become confident in her own ability
* encourage her powers of observation, understanding and sense of humour.

When your child is ready and keen to learn to read (a Reading Readiness checklist is given in the Parent/Teacher Guide*) introduce this book just like any other picture storybook. Find a quiet, comfortable place and either read the book all the way through or read and talk about one page at a time. Point to the words and show that reading goes from left to right.*

---

* To avoid the clumsy he/she, him/her, we have referred to the child as ''she''.
All the books are of course equally suited to both boys and girls.

READ with me! *has been written using about 800 words and these include the 300 Key Words.*

In the first six books, all words introduced occur again in the following book to provide vital repetition in the early stages. The number of new words increases as the child gains confidence and progresses through the stories.

After Book 6, a wider range of vocabulary is used but each word is repeated at least three times within that story.

The stories centre on the everyday lives of Kate, Tom, Sam the dog, Mum, Dad, friends, neighbours and relations. This setting often provides a springboard into Tom and Kate's world of make-believe. Also, the humorous, colourful illustrations include picture story sequences to stimulate the reader's own language and imagination.

A complete list of stories is given on the back cover and suggestions for using each book are made on the back pages.

Further details about this reading scheme plus a card listing the 300 Key Words are contained in the Parent/Teacher Guide.

This book belongs to

_____

_____

British Library Cataloguing in Publication Data
Murray, W. (William) *(date)*
  Kate and the crocodile.
  1. English language—Readers
  I. Title   II. Corby, Jill   III. Trotter, Stuart   IV. Series
  428.6
  ISBN 0-7214-1318-8

First edition

Published by Ladybird Books Ltd Loughborough Leicestershire UK
Ladybird Books Inc Auburn Maine 04210 USA

Printed in England